This book belongs to

_____

ISBN-10: 1699278679
ISBN-13: 978-1699278673

www.johnoboyle.net

Written by John O'Boyle

Cover art and original black and white
interior illustrations by Mykita Harets
ngarets@gmail.com

Edited by Shannon Jade
www.wildflowerbooks.net

Thank you to Moira for the interior illustration colouring.

The Christmas Eve Crash Landing

written by

John O'Boyle

illustrated by

Mykyta Harets

Get free colouring and activity sheets at

www.johnoboyle.net

It was the night before Christmas; I was ready for bed.

I was really excited; festive thoughts filled my head.

I knew it was bedtime when my Mum appeared.

"One more sleep," she said smiling, "then Christmas is here."

I could see Dad outside as we walked through the hall.
"Dad's fixing the car," said Mum, "it's not working at all.
He should see a mechanic. It's what I'd recommend.
But your Dad says there's nothing a hammer can't mend."

A few hours later I was sound asleep, snoring.

I woke with a fright. I heard a man roaring.

"Brace for impact!" he shouted. "We're going down fast!"

I was sure I heard sleigh bells as something flew past.

I jumped out of bed, all thoughts of sleep gone.

Mum and Dad had to know that something was wrong.

They were both in the kitchen. I burst in from the hall.

And that's when I realised...

Suddenly, the back door was flung open wide.

Then a big bearded jolly man swaggered inside.

"Santa, it's you!" I cried, smiling with joy.

In a deep voice he said, "In the flesh, my dear boy!"

"My sleigh just lost power. I had to crash land.
I really would love you to lend me a hand.
It's quite complex, though. It's a tricky invention.
If I can borrow a tool box, I'll check over the engine."

"An engine?" I asked, "can't your reindeer all fly?"

He said, "They're mostly for show. They look good in the sky.

It's a very long night, and they sometimes get lazy.

With no engine for backup, I'd breach Elfin Safety!"

Always make sure sack is secure before take-off.

The sleigh must always fly with a working backup engine on Christmas Eve.

Too many carrots can cause severe reindeer flatulence.

I went for the tool box; Santa looked on, approving.

"Santa," I said, "my parents aren't moving."

"Oh yes," Santa smiled, "don't worry, they're fine.

What you might not have known is that I can freeze time."

"It's a trick I use," said Santa, "as I travel the world.
It's how, in one night, I visit all the boys and girls.
I didn't freeze you, because I needed a hand.
They'll go back to normal once I'm gone, understand?"

I put on my jacket, and we both went outside.

I stopped in my tracks and stood, eyes opened wide.

Santa's sleigh was in my garden! It was red with gold trim.

And eight wonderful reindeer, standing proudly for him.

Santa opened a panel on the back of the sled.
He looked over the engine and then shook his head.
"The compressor is fine, and I've checked the cam sprocket.
And it looks like the filter is tight in the socket."

"What could it be?" Santa wondered, scratching his head.
That's when I remembered what Dad always said.
"Santa," I asked, tapping him on the back, "have you tried
just giving the engine a whack?"

"What harm could it do?" he replied with a grin.

I pulled out the hammer and passed it to him.

He lifted it up, high over his head.

"Just in case this goes wrong, stand back!" Santa said.

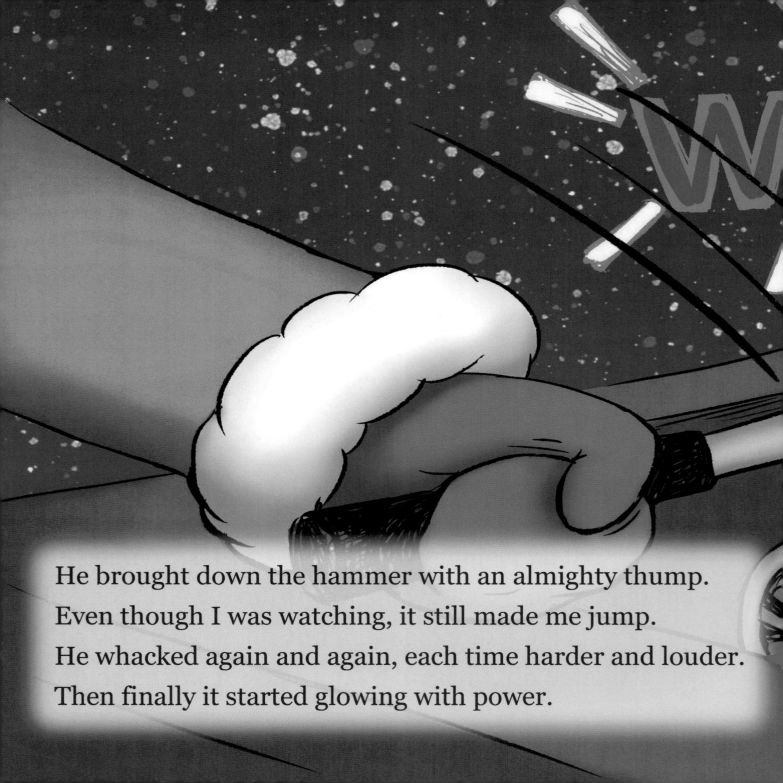

He brought down the hammer with an almighty thump.
Even though I was watching, it still made me jump.
He whacked again and again, each time harder and louder.
Then finally it started glowing with power.

"It worked!" Santa cheered. "The engine's alive!"

He held up his hand so that we could high five.

"Now I really do need to be on my way.

I hope you know you just saved Christmas Day!"

"One more thing," Santa added, putting his hand on
my shoulder. "I'm afraid you won't remember tonight
when you're older. Part of my magic makes you forget
that I've been. And tomorrow you'll think
this was all just a dream."

He jumped into his sleigh and pulled on the reigns.

The reindeer got ready; blood pumped through their veins.

"On Dasher! On Dancer! Oh, you know the rest!

It's been a tough night, so just do your best!"

The engine hummed nicely; they rose to the sky.

"Thanks for your help!" Santa called as he waved me goodbye.

They zoomed past the moon, as fast as a rocket.

Then I remembered the hammer was still in his pocket.

The next thing I remember was waking in bed.
"It was a dream," I said sadly, shaking my head.
"Merry Christmas!" cheered Mum, coming into my room.
"Get up, sleepy head. It's breakfast time soon."

And then Dad walked in with a letter in his hand.

"I found this outside," he said, "but I don't understand."

I opened the letter, and I had to read it twice...

It said...

ISBN-10: 1699278673
ISBN-13: 978-1699278673

www.johnorme.net

Written by John O'Boyle

Cover art and original black and white
interior illustrations by Mykie
rgarets@gmail.com

Edited by Shannon Jade
www.wildflowerbooks.net

Thank you to Moira for the in

Thank you for supporting an independent author!

Book reviews play a huge part in helping independent books reach a wider audience. If you liked this book, please consider taking a few minutes to review it on Amazon.

You can get free colouring and activity sheets at my website, as well as being able to sign up to hear about new book releases early (and win free copies).

www.johnoboyle.net

Email me at john@johnoboyle.net

Connect with me on social media

Twitter: @JoboyleAuthor

Facebook: fb.me/JoboyleAuthor

Instagram.com/johnobwrites

Contact the illustrator:
Mykita Harets
ngarets@gmail.com

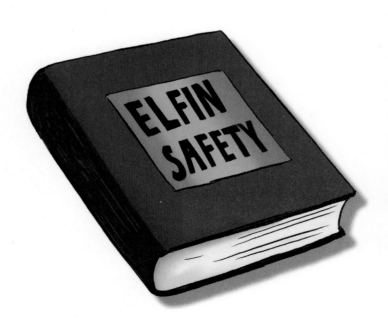

Printed in Great Britain
by Amazon

11530860R00029